Produced by Kroha Associates, Inc.
Middletown, Connecticut.
Printed in the United States of America.
ISBN 1-56326-105-7

Pops For Penny

By Ruth Lerner Perle

Minnie and Penny loved to go to the shopping mall together. They liked to ride the escalators and watch the changing colors of the indoor water fountain. But mostly, they liked to look in the store windows.

One afternoon when Minnie and Penny were at the mall, Minnie said, "I can't wait until we're grown up. Then we'll be able to buy lots of things."

"Yes," Penny said. "I wish we could have anything we wanted."

Minnie and Penny stopped in front of the toy store. There were dozens of beautiful dolls and a trunk full of doll clothes in the window.

"Aren't those dolls great?" Minnie said.

"Yes, they're really nice!" Penny agreed. "Let's go in and look at them."

They opened the door and went inside.

Minnie and Penny headed straight for the aisle where the dolls were. They saw baby dolls, rag dolls, antique dolls, and dolls that could cry and close their eyes. But the doll both girls liked best had long hair and special outfits for all kinds of occasions.

Minnie held their favorite doll in her hands. "If I had lots of money, I would buy this doll and I'd get all these different clothes for her," she said.

Penny held up a tiny comb and brush set. "I'd love to have this set to use on my dolls at home," she said.

"So would I," Minnie agreed.

It sure would be nice to have these pretty things. It's too bad we can't always have everything we want.

Minnie put the doll back on the shelf, and the girls left the store. As they continued walking through the mall, they smelled something delicious in the air. It was a sweet, chocolate smell.

"Mmm, mmm! Do you smell what I smell?" Minnie said. She took Penny's hand and together they followed the smell around the corner to a big stand selling giant chocolate chip cookies and all kinds of lollipops. There was a long line of people waiting their turn to buy a treat. Minnie and Penny went to the counter to take a closer look.

"Yummy!" Penny cried. "I wish we could have one of those big cookies and a chocolate lollipop."

Minnie looked in her purse. "I have enough money for a cookie or a lollipop, but not both," she said. "The cookie is big enough for us to share, so let's buy that."

Penny looked at the lollipops. She smiled a funny smile.
"I think I know how we can have a cookie *and* a lollipop!"
she whispered to Minnie.

Penny looked around to make sure no one saw her. Then she reached for one of the lollipops.

"Oh, Penny!" Minnie said. "Don't do that! You can't take a lollipop without paying for it!"

"But no one will see me!" Penny said.

Minnie put her money back in her purse and pulled Penny away from the stand. Then the girls went to a nearby bench and sat down.

"What's the matter?" Penny asked. "It's just a silly old lollipop."

"It's not right to take things that don't belong to you," said Minnie.

"But nobody would have seen me," Penny said.

"It doesn't matter if nobody else knows. You'll know you did something wrong and you won't feel right inside."

PERSONALIZED
-UDGE LOLLIPOPS
WHILE YOU WAIT-

Penny's eyes filled with tears. "Oh, Minnie, now I do feel awful!" she cried.

"Don't cry, Penny," Minnie said, handing her a tissue. "You may have wanted to take that lollipop, but you didn't. You didn't do anything wrong. You should feel glad, not sad."

"But you don't understand!" Penny said. "I did do something wrong. I did take something that doesn't belong to me. Come with me and I'll show you."

Penny led Minnie behind a big plant next to the fountain. When she was sure no one was looking, she reached into her pocket and pulled out a small package. It was the little comb and brush set! "Oh, no!" cried Minnie. "You took that from the toy store!"

"I don't feel right inside, just like you said," Penny cried. "I know what I did was wrong, but I don't know what to do next."

"The only thing to do is to return the set to the store," Minnie said.

Minnie took Penny's hand and together they walked back to the toy store.

A salesman was standing near the door. "Yes, young ladies," he said. "What can I do for you?"

"Well, er, that is," stammered Penny.

"Yes? What is it?" the man said.

Penny took the package out of her pocket and handed it to the man. "I want to return this to you. I took it by mistake," she said.

The salesman smiled. "There's no need to return this! These packages are free gifts — samples of our new toy line. You're very welcome to them."

Penny could hardly believe her ears. She was so relieved!

When the girls were out in the mall again, Penny said, "Wow! I really learned my lesson about taking things that don't belong to you. I feel so much better now."

The two friends sat down on a bench. Minnie smiled and said, "I'm glad everything turned out all right, Penny. Now I have something to do. Wait here and I'll be right back."

Before long, Minnie came running over carrying a paper bag.
She smiled and gave it to Penny.

Inside the bag was a great big, heart-shaped, fudge lollipop wrapped in cellophane. There was a message written on it in pink icing: *WITH LOVE TO PENNY.*

Then Minnie said, "I'm so proud of you, Penny. What you did today was very brave."

Penny smiled. "Thank you, Minnie, for being such a good friend! You're always there when I need you!" Then the two friends enjoyed the special treat together.